The Hole

The Hole

José Revueltas

introduction
by Álvaro Enrigue

translated
by Amanda Hopkinson
& Sophie Hughes

A NEW DIRECTIONS PAPERBOOK ORIGINAL

The Hole was originally published as *El apando* in 1969 by Ediciones
Era, Mexico.

First published as New Directions Paperbook 1426 in 2018
Manufactured in the United States of America
New Directions Books are printed on acid-free paper
Design by Erik Rieselbach

Library of Congress Cataloging-in-Publication Data
Names: Revueltas, Josâe, 1914–1976, author. | Enrigue, Alvaro, 1969–
writer of introduction. | Hopkinson, Amanda, 1948– translator. |
Hughes, Sophie (Sophie Elizabeth), 1986– translator.
Title: The hole / by Jose Revueltas ; introduction by Alvaro Enrigue ;
translated by Amanda Hopkinson and Sophie Hughes.
Other titles: Apando. English
Description: New York, NY : New Directions Publishing, 2018.
Identifiers: LCCN 2018021047 (print) | LCCN 2018024712 (ebook) |
ISBN 9780811227797 (ebook) | ISBN 9780811227780 (alk. paper)
Subjects: LCSH: Prisoners—Fiction. | Drug addiction—Fiction. |
Mexico—Fiction.
Classification: LCC PQ7297.R383 (ebook) | LCC PQ7297.R383 A813 2018
(print) | DDC 863/.64—dc23
LC record available at https://lccn.loc.gov/2018021047

10 9 8 7 6 5 4 3 2 1

New Directions Books are published for James Laughlin
by New Directions Publishing Corporation
80 Eighth Avenue, New York 10011

to Pablo Neruda

CONTENTS

INTRODUCTION

The Hole begins with the description of what an eye sees through a confined space: the small hatch of a punishment cell that opens onto the corridors of Lecumberri Prison in Mexico City. *The Hole* is at once a piece of fiction and a deposition: José Revueltas wrote it between February and March of 1969, while in jail for participating in the 1968 student movement.

Revueltas was not a student in the late 1960s. He was then fifty-four years old and, in fact, had never attended university: in 1932, when he was seventeen and should have been thinking about college, he was already serving his second term in prison, as a result of his militancy in the then illegal Communist Party of Mexico.

By the late sixties Revueltas was a well-known leftist writer and activist with views that suited the Student Movement's demands for a less vertical government, having maintained his vocal social-ist advocacy and strong links to the trade-union movement, while at the same time vigorously denouncing both the Institutional Revolutionary Party's government (which had ruled the coun-try with absolute authority for more than forty years) and the Mexican totalitarian Stalinist orga-nizations that opposed it. The students considered him a natural ally: the weight of his reputation of-fered credible ideological shelter for a movement demanding respect for civil liberties and fresh at-tention to the perennial problem of inequality in Mexico.

The place of *The Hole's* creation is important. Lecumberri Prison, where the manuscript is dated, is an outsized symbol in the Mexican imagination. It was inaugurated in 1900 as a triumphant dem-onstration of the "progressive" rationalist ideol-ogy that dominated the government's discourse at the turn of the twentieth century. Porfirio Díaz, the liberal dictator who ruled the country with an iron fist from 1884 to 1911, built the prison to keep all opposition to his regime locked up and under close scrutiny in more or less humanitarian conditions; designed by the architect Miguel Macedo, it adopted Jeremy Bentham's model of the panopticon—as set out in his letters from Russia in 1797.

According to Bentham—whose works Revueltas, well versed in political philosophy, had no doubt read—the panopticon is simultaneously a jail and a theater. The greater the visibility of its inmates, the greater the benefit a society obtains from their punishment, which keeps the prisoners out of circulation while transforming them into an example and a spectacle. At the center of Lecumberri Prison was a watchtower from which seven wings radiated outward, every one constantly visible from its hub.

When the long and bloody Revolution against Porfirio Díaz's regime finally succeeded in installing a stable government (if in the form of a party dictatorship), the prison continued fulfilling its primary purpose as a space of atonement for political opponents—now of the nationalist revolutionary government. By 1929, Lecumberri's architect, Miguel Macedo, was occupying a cell in his own building, having been deemed a collaborator of the previous, ousted régime: getting locked up in Lecumberri implied being a victim of a political purge, but also, above all, playing a leading role in the spectacle of public punishment.

As the twentieth century advanced, the prison became more crowded—and over-crowded—with petty criminals, even though it also continued to host the opponents of every successive political régime until it was finally closed in 1976. Its looming shadow over Mexico is such that even today people still refer to the building as "the Black Palace"—as if the mere mention of its real name might bring misfortune—despite the fact that it's not black at all and, since 1980, has been the seat of the National Archives.

Such is the general context of *The Hole* as it opens with an eye peering at a piece of this panopticon. The author's intentions are clear right from the start: Revueltas's fable is a meditation on the way contemporary societies make a performance out of punishment. He portrays prison life as an avant-garde production, where Antonin Artaud's Theater of Cruelty and Jean Genet's Theater of Hatred intersect.

What the prisoner's eye sees in the first pages of *The Hole* is a glimpse of two floors of cells in the jail's wing hosting common criminals. The eye belongs to Polonio, the tale's main character, who is busily calculating how long it takes the guards to make their rounds through the corridors as he waits for a package of drugs to be delivered from the outside.

Revueltas, it should be said, was a special case: he was never in the hole, and unlike many of those detained after the 1968 student uprising, he was never disappeared or tortured, presumably because he was an intellectual celebrity. On top of that, "Revueltas" was a name with public resonance, well known to artistic circles in Mexico and around the world. José's older brother, Silvestre, an important composer during the first half of the twentieth century, had a close, collaborative friendship with Aaron Copland and Leonard Bernstein; Fermín, the second brother, a prominent muralist, had his work displayed in many government buildings. Rosaura Revueltas, José's sister, had her Hollywood career as an actress cut short in 1954 when her name appeared on Senator McCarthy's blacklist during the filming of *The Salt of the*

Earth. Despite the relatively good treatment the novelist received in Lecumberri, he'd been placed in the common criminals' wing at the start of his sentence, maybe because the prison governor regarded him as an ideologue and preferred to keep him separate from the rest of the political prisoners, mainly the students who revered him.

There's a photograph of Revueltas, a half smile on his face, right next to a punishment cell, which offers useful information about the story's setting. A Lecumberri "hole" was a long and narrow passageway, with cement floors and walls, blocked at one end by a metal door with a hatch in its middle, more or less chest-high. The holes looked like containers to transport cattle. A barred window, far up in one wall, was the only source of light. The hatch, just large enough for a soup plate and a cup to be passed through, had a little door that opened outward and could be propped halfway up to serve as a tray for handing in the prisoners' dishes. Anyone inside the hole wanting to look out needed to stick whatever would fit of his head through the open hatch: this is Polonio's position when the story begins, and what he is seeing are the "monos."

In 1960s Mexican prison slang, a guard was a "mono"—a word that, depending on the context, might mean an ape, a nobody, or a character in a comic strip. Polonio sees the monos ("the apes" in Amanda Hopkinson and Sophie Hughes's brave and polished English translation) making their rounds and Revueltas fully employs the term's multiple associations to shift the story's initial image to the world's origins, in both the scientific and sacred senses. The guards might be apes trapped "on the zoological scale," but are also the founding couple of a subverted Eden of nobodies: "he-apes and she-apes in Paradise." As they move, framed by the box of the hatch, they appear to the reader as Expressionist comic illustrations—like Adam and Eve, but primitive and cartoonish.

This opening sequence reveals the author's approach to the art of telling: a concept is distilled from a scene and then sublimated to produce a literary judgment on the limited condition of the characters: in the beginning there was abjection and the Word was full of scorn. A meditation on the despair of the human condition can be extracted from this scenario. And it is reiterated throughout the whole

first half of the story in which nothing occurs beyond awaiting delivery of a package of drugs.

Polonio is not alone in the hole: Albino and
The Prick are there, and also, like him, come from
the most wretched depths of Mexican society. All
three are awaiting the arrival of visitors: The Prick's
mother, and the girlfriends of Polonio and Albino—the barely adolescent Meche and la Chata.
The three women have to get from the prison en-
trance to the hole, and, once there, the girls will
create a commotion to distract the guards, allowing
the old woman to hand over the heroin.

The novel's plot—unfolding in real time, exactly
as long as it takes to read—opens at the precise
moment the female visitors enter the prison com-
plex. They have to cross several barriers, submit
to extensive searches by the female guards, and
then wait with the rest of the visitors to enter the
common prisoners wing. The final holding area is
a quad, barred on all sides, which will play a vital
role in the resolution of the novel. For the three
prisoners in the hole—all of them going through
withdrawal—the women appear to be moving
along their route at the speed of tectonic plates.

José Revueltas's gaze functioned like a CAT scan—what everyone usually sees is here only outlined: what his writing shows is everything beating within the organism itself. Maybe all literary writing operates the same way—I recount A in order to say B—but Revueltas habitually inverted the realist equation popularized in the novels of the nineteenth century, primarily the French and Russian ones, or those drawn from the Mexican Revolution, which had formed his horizon as a reader. He wrote of what he saw, devoting attention to verisimilitude, but what he cared about was not the perceptible, but what lies behind that. He used conventional narrative strategies, but also a voice that is constantly thinking about what's being told.

In addition, as a keen and confirmed Marxist—despite his reservations regarding the way that the Communist parties of his time applied the notion of the Dictatorship of the Proletariat—he perceived economic and political forces driving history where the rest of us see individuals in action. For this reason, his writing has an illuminated quality, a biblical flavor, in spite of the fact that he was a raging atheist. His style was always drawn toward the future, toward what would happen once history itself was ending. Revueltas acted and wrote like a prophet—but a prophet from a Political Science department, sporting a beard like Trotsky's.

At the very middle of the novel, the three female characters finally enter Polonio's field of vision, shifting the narrative from the hole and the characters' interior lives to the chaotic world of the prison. Time, moving with grinding slowness up to this point, turns back on itself, transforming into a whirlwind.

In a January 11, 1970, letter to Arthur Miller, Revueltas, a fellow senior member of PEN international, described a terrifying assault in Lecumberri: on New Year's Eve 1969, the common prisoners broke the police cordon and attacked the wing of activists and students. The assault, so savage and unexpected, was perceived by the political prisoners as a moment of concentrated reality: "Things," he wrote to Miller, "occurred with precipitate, fantastical, and dreamlike speed." I cannot find a more concise way to describe the tumult provoked by the women once they reach the hole, things precipitating with brutal speed. What had always been the same is broken and, after that rupture, reality itself undergoes a process of intensification, dropping the astonished characters into a nightmare.

As I write this introduction, I experience a pang of envy when I consider that the English reader is about to encounter, for the first time, the final twenty pages of *The Hole*, one of the greatest pieces of twentieth-century writing composed in Spanish. The symbolic content that Revueltas poured into the first part erupts on all sides. Everything is atrociously real, saturated with meaning, even as the spiraling vortex of images exposes the blinding banality of violence when it becomes an end in itself. The novel does not invite empathy, any more than it allows for pity or even solidarity, since by distancing itself morally from the characters, Revueltas's criticism turns in on itself: it's true that both the guards and the prisoners "in the hole" are "homicidal to the roots of their hair," but it's the class that owns the means of production—to which the author who is giving testimony belongs—that has alienated them to the point of becoming beasts.

The Hole is the collision of a thriller and a meditation on political philosophy, existing between two opposing linguistic registers—that of the prisoners and that of the narrator—which expose the ruptures in society as a whole. It reads with the high-speed intensity of a crime novel: Revueltas, though deeply ideological, understood the limits of Marxism as a creative form of expression. He had such a mocking and black sense of humor that—though it made for political difficulties (surely he set the world record for expulsions from Communist organizations)— his writing remained always free of the servility that destroyed the literary ambitions of two or three generations of radical Latin American novelists.

Maintaining his sense of humor and literary imagination even in the direst circumstances, Revueltas, while still detained in Lecumberri's wing reserved for murderers—he was only transferred to another wing with the rest of the political prisoners a year later, following a hunger strike—sent a letter on December 7, 1968, to his protégé Martín Dozal, imprisoned with the students. It was to be read aloud to his fellow inmates, announcing that he was soon due to receive a typewriter, something that would facilitate communication with his comrades in the struggle. "From then on," he noted, mocking the Marxist jargon of the students' committees, "there will be a marked improvement in my calligraphical superstructure."

This sense of humor, as corrosive as it was intolerable to the hard-line Communists of his time, brought with it an infinite number of problems—which is probably the reason why, outside Mexico, he still remains mostly unknown: he was simply too much for the loftiest figures of the international left.

When Revueltas published his first novel, *Walls of Water*, Pablo Neruda denounced it for its pessimism: such existentialist themes were disrespectful of Stalinist orthodoxy. Neruda failed to understand the literary potential of young José Revueltas, who in turn held the Chilean poet—the loftiest of all lofty Communists—in such high esteem that he took *Walls of Water* off the market. Nevertheless, Neruda was correct in pointing out the link between Revueltas and post-war French literature. His tragic characters belong to the race of Albert Camus's existential heroes: "indifferent to the future."

The ending of *The Hole*, stripped of all theatricality despite being intensely tragic and brutally comic in its existential way, can only be fully understood by recognizing that Polonio's "Why bother" echoes Meursault's indifference in the face of his own death at the end of *L'Étranger*. Those in the hole are visionaries with both feet planted beyond the limits, creatures beside themselves, like Jean Genet's martyrs of Modernity.

The Hole might be only a well-written prison story were it not for Revueltas's sophisticated play with the point of view of the narrator, who is never seen but judges the events which are all told in his cynical, intensely literary voice. The panopticon alienates the lower class to the extent of erasing its humanity—in this tale there's no difference between the prisoners and their guards—but the most abject among these brutalized characters are busy testing the limits: there's something enterprising and adventurous in their barbarism. On the other hand, the narrator—an outsider to this violence who gives the novel's testimony thanks to the fact that his social class owns the grammar and the vocabulary, the syntax and the reference book of Western culture—has become even less human than his characters. He merely reports on the horror out of curiosity.

His account demonstrates that barbarism exists, but also explains why: the writer owns the fruits of his labor and the very act of conveying a battle of the lesser members of the society through language shows that some get the suffering while others benefit from it. Revueltas's narrator regards the gladiators as savages who lack all moral scruples simply because he can: the master of the grammatical rules that shape society's norms (integral to authority), he is there to narrate the theater of the panopticon as the public applauds from the outside.

A Christological reading of the novel's Expressionist ending—"lines and more lines, bars and more bars ... the monstrous blueprint of this gargantuan defeat of liberty, all the fault of geometry"—is inevitable: Revueltas himself uses *crucified* to describe how the prisoners are ultimately subjugated. An April 5, 1969, journal entry from the author (twenty days after he finished writing the book) suggests, however, a different reading of these mysterious final pages: "An invisible web of fiction surrounds us and we struggle as prisoners inside it like those who struggle to free themselves from a spider's web from which there is no escape." This fiction that secures us as in a spider web is the whole political system — and its masters, us, the owners of speech, should be held responsible for the inequality it produces even when our acts are generally well intended and harmless. There is no way out, but there is a thread to follow: imagining a justice system that could do without the spectacle of punishment.

The publication of *The Hole* in the United States at this precise moment in time could not be more pertinent: it's a perfect fable about our complicity — all writers and readers — in the triumph of mass incarceration as the only solution to problems that could be resolved in more rational ways.

Everybody knows that jail doesn't help reintegrate those who have renounced the pursuit of society's norms; it only serves as a spectacle that feeds our leisure hours with the newspaper and television — the panopticon that we contemplate as evidence of our moral superiority. In a country and an era of unparalleled imprisonment we are all, along with the novel's narrator, an amused audience, a bunch of cold witnesses. We are accomplices and we are all directly compromised.

—ÁLVARO ENRIGUE

TRANSLATED BY AMANDA HOPKINSON

THE HOLE

They were captive there, the apes, just like the rest, male and female; or rather, male and male, the pair of them in their cage, not quite despairing, not yet totally desperate, pacing from one side to the other, detained but in motion, trapped on the zoological scale as if someone, the others, all humanity, had irreverently washed their hands of the matter, this matter of them being apes, which they to wanted to forget, apes when all's said and done, who didn't or refused to get it, captive whichever way you looked at them, penned in that two-story-high barred cage, in their blue uniforms with shining badges on their heads, in their unregimented to- and fro-ing, easy and yet fixed, never managing to take the one step that would allow them to emerge from their interspecies, where they moved, walked, copulated, cruel and lacking all recollection, he-apes and she-apes in Paradise, identical, same hair, same sex, but male and female, imprisoned, fucked. His head carefully and expertly cocked to press his left ear against the horizontal metal sheet that closed the narrow hatch, Polonio squinted down on them from above, his right eye looking along the sharp line of his nose, watching how they paced from one side to the other, the bunch of keys hanging from their blue cloth jackets, jangling against their thighs to the swing of each step. First one then the other, the two apes were sized up, monitored from the second floor by that head with just one eye to observe them, the head on Salome's platter, poking out of the hatch, the talking fairground head, detached from the torso—like at the fair, the head that tells the future and recites rhymes, John the Baptist's head, only in this case tilted sideways, resting on its ear—preventing the left eye from seeing anything below, just the surface of the metal sheet that sealed the hatch, while the apes, in the cage, crossed paths as they paced from one end to the other, and that talking head—delivering insults in a long, slow, plangent, cynical drawl, dragging out the vowels on a wave of something like a melody of jarring alternate accents—told them to go fuck their mothers each time either one of them moved into his good eye's field of vision. "Those fucking *ape* sons of bitches." They were captive. More captive than Polonio, more captive than Albino, more captive than the Prick. For a few seconds it was empty, that rectangular cage, the apes disappearing momentarily as they paced back and forth in opposite directions to the far walls of the cage—thirty meters or so, sixty there and back—and that virgin, formless space transformed into inalienable sovereign territory under Polonio's stubborn right eye, which took in, millimeter by millimeter, each and every detail of that section of the wing. Apes, *arch*-apes, stupid, vile, and naïve, naïve as a ten-year-old whore. So stupid they didn't seem to notice that they alone were the captives, they and their mothers and their children and their forefathers. They were born to keep watch and they knew as much, to spy, to constantly look around, making sure no one escaped their clutches in that city with its iron grid of streets, barred corridors, corners multiplying on all sides, and that stupid face they wore was nothing but the manifestation of a certain, hazy longing for other unattainable aptitudes, a certain stutter of the soul in their simian features, underlaid with grief for an irremediable loss of which they remained ignorant, eyes all over them, a mesh of eyes covering their bodies, a river of pupils rushing over their limbs, napes, necks, arms, chests, balls, all to put food on the table at home, or so they told themselves, where their ape families danced and screeched—the little boys and girls and the wife, hairy on the inside— during their twenty-four long hours with the master ape at home, after his twenty-four hour shift in the penitentiary, stretched out on the bed, foul and clammy, the grease-smeared banknotes from petty bribes laying on the bedside table, but never leaving the prison, vile and captive in an endless circulation, ape-notes, which the wife repeatedly smoothed and pressed in the palm of her hand, slowly, terribly, not knowing what she was doing. Life was one long not knowing anything at all: not

knowing that there they were in their cage, husband and wife, husband and husband, wife and
children, father and father, sons and fathers, terri-
fied, universal apes. The Prick begged to watch
them from the hatch, too. Polonio could think of
nothing but how vile it was to have the Prick there,
just as caged, just as *holed*. "You know you can't,
man...!" He spoke in the same long, rolling ca-
dences he used to abuse the guards in their box,
one voice and yet indifferent, used by all like a personal trademark, and which, whether blindly or
merely in the dark, didn't much help to tell them
apart, except for the fact that it was the kind of
voice that oozed smug complacency and a sense of
superiority and hierarchy upheld by a certain class
oblivious of what thugs they really were. Of course
he couldn't. Not because of the skill it required to
place your head through the hatch and position it
there, at an angle, ears catching as it slid across the
metal sheet to rest on Salome's platter, but because
the Prick was missing his right eye, and with the
left one alone he wouldn't see a thing apart from
the metal surface, close up, coarse, abrasive — and
well, that's why they called him the Prick, for being

such a useless prick, blind in one eye, dragging himself around with the shakes and a lame leg, no dignity at all, known throughout the Penitentiary for his habit of carving up his veins each time he was banged up in the *hole*, his forearms covered in laddered scars like a guitar fretboard, as if he were beyond desperate—but no, he never killed himself—forsaken, sunk, always on edge, not giving a damn about the body that didn't seem to belong to him, yet a body that he relished, safeguarded, and inside which he hid, appropriating it fiercely with urgent, restless fervor whenever he was able to possess it, climbing inside, all the way down, to lie in its abyss, flooded by a warm, unguent pleasure, climbing inside his own corporeal cage, the drug like a faceless white angel leading him by the hand through rivers of blood, as if he were coursing through an infinite palace with no rooms and no echoes. The goddamn disgrace of a mother who bore him. "I'm telling you, you can't, man. Get off my fucking back!" Despite everything, the Prick's mother was due to visit, she existed, however inconceivable her existence. During visiting hours— in a narrow, irregularly shaped room, filled with

benches and hordes of people, inmates and relatives, where it was easy to pick out the lawyers and
(easier still) the con men, recognizable by their
poise and the excessively cunning airs they assumed as they studied a particular document, af-
fecting a dumb ponderousness as their words
slipped into their clients' ears, and as they shot
rapid and deliberately suspicious glances at the
door (one of numerous ruses to bolster their clients' trust and, simultaneously, their sense of be-
musement)—during these interviews, the Prick's
mother—amazingly just as ugly as her son, a knife
scar running from her eyebrow to the tip of her
chin—kept her head down, not looking at him or
anything else, only at the floor, her bearing laden
with resentment, reproach, and regret, God only
knows under what sordid and abject conditions
she'd coupled, or with whom, in order to engender
him, and perhaps the memory of that distant, grim
deed still tormented her each time. Every now and
then she'd let out a heavy, rasping sigh. "It's *no-
oneses* fault, *no-oneses* but mine for having had
you." The word *no-ones* had become etched in Polonio's memory, strange and curious, as if it were

the sum of an infinite number of meanings. *No-ones*, that sad plural. It was *no-oneses* fault, just fate's, life's, damned misfortune's, *no-oneses*. For having had you. The rage at having the Prick banged up beside them now in the same cell, right beside Polonio and Albino, and the acute, urgent, craven desire for him to die once and for all, to cease roaming the earth in that debased body of his. His mother desired it too, just as deeply, just as keenly, you could tell. Die die die. He inspired livid, revulsion-fueled compassion. Nothing ever came of his vein cutting, nothing but ranting and raving, despite their hoping, genuinely and devoutly, every time, that he'd finish the job. He would cower by the cell door—any given day, any day he spent banged up in the *hole*—deliberately against the doorframe, so that the runnel of blood welling up from his vein would flow out as soon as possible into the narrow hallway, on the wing's upper floor, and from there drip down onto the yard, forming a puddle on the concrete; having worked out how long it would take for all this to happen, the Prick could be sure they would get wise to his suicide and he'd howl like a dog, his breath squeezed through a broken bellow, never dying, just enough to cause a scene so they'd take him from the *hole* to the infirmary where he'd find a way to wangle more drugs, setting off the cycle all over again, a hundred, a thousand times, never reaching the end before he found himself in the next *hole.* It was on one such occasion that he and Polonio first met, the Prick dancing a kind of semi-orthopedic jig halfway up a footpath in the infirmary garden, tripping over his tongue as he reeled off verses from the Bible. Around his neck he wore a tie fashioned from a greasy length of cord, and through the rags of his blue jacket, as his dance evolved, you caught flashes of his naked chest and torso, scored with barbaric scars and faded tattoos showing beneath his skin. His good eye and the flower were stomach turning, bloodcurdling: the flower was new, freshly picked, a mutilated gladiola missing some petals, fastened by a piece of rusty wire to the tatters of his jacket, and there, beneath his drooping, half-shut eyelid, which had no lashes at all, his good eye was glazed over with a malicious, calculating, mocking, self-pitying, and tender look. He bent his good leg, the lame one stood to attention, and with his hands on his hips and his feet turned out in that squatting pose of erotic dancers from old illustrated magazines, he attempted a few short jerks forward, during which he lost his balance and fell to the floor, where he tried to get up, writhing and kicking furiously, sending himself spinning on the spot, without it occurring to anyone to come to his aid. At that point his good eye seemed to die on him, as still and artificial as a bird's. It was with this eye that he kept his mother under observation during visiting hours, not breathing a word. Beyond a doubt she wished him dead, perhaps because of that eye in which she herself was dead, but in the meantime she got him his drug money, twenty, fifty pesos, and she would sit there, having passed it to him—the notes scrunched into a ball like a candy, sticky and sweaty in the hollow of her fist— across the bench in the visitors' room, her worm-filled belly like a bundle of laundry slumped over her stumpy legs, which didn't quite touch the floor, hermetic and supernatural in the interminable pain of bearing this son who still clung to her entrails, where he watched her with his miscreant's eye, refusing to leave the womb, trapped in the amniotic sac, in his cell, surrounded by bars, by *apes*, of which he was one, propelling himself in circles, always with that one eye of his, powerless to get up from the floor, like a bird with one wing, powerless to leave his mother's belly, banged up inside his mother's hole. Since this was more or less the plan, and Polonio was its mastermind, it fell to him to convince her; in the end—without much difficulty—she consented. "You're a woman of a certain age, mature, respected. The bitches don't dare try any funny business with you." The thing was just there, *inside* her, something maternal. Polonio described it as a cotton plug attached to a thread about twelve inches long, its end dangling loose, a tip to pull the thing out after the event—all the rage these days among women— and it was merely a question of Mecha and La Chata talking her through it, assisting her, so they wouldn't wind up pregnant only to have to get rid of the child in some horrible manner, one of the latest methods, Mecha or La Chata would explain everything and help her put it up there nice and snug. In there everything *died*, in there spermatozoa became trapped, condemned to death, wild and raging at the barrier, banging on the door just like the guards, apes just like the rest of them—an endless throng of apes banging on locked doors. Polonio hooted with laughter and the two women, Meche and La Chata, did the same, thrilled by how *ballsy* the old girl had been to accept. But then: of course it hadn't occurred to anyone that the mother might want to take the chance to use it for any other purpose, to put it like that. The makeshift tampon, tied nice and firmly in a knot, would contain some twenty or thirty grams of drugs, which the other two girls would hand over to the Prick's mother. "The *bitches* have never tried it on with you, right? Because you're a woman in your prime, well respected. Not like us. When they pat us down they always slip the finger in, filthy *bitches*." The memory and the idea and the image all made Polonio blind with jealousy, with a strange, absolute jealousy, a kind of incapacity for existing in his own space, for recognizing himself or feeling the limits of his own body, vague, bereft, jealousy in his throat and the pit of his stomach, and a faint and terrible tingling sensation behind his penis, it felt like a premature ejaculation, as opposed to a real one, a kind of contact without semen, which fluttered, vibrated in tiny microscopic, tangible circles, beyond the body, beyond any organism at all, and there before his eyes La Chata would appear, jocund, bestial, and the lines of her thighs, which, when she stood upright, instead of coming together to form the cradle of her sex, left a small gap between the two walls of solid, firm, young, heart-rending flesh. Seen through her dress, backlit — and now Polonio was struck by a vivid rush of nostalgia, from the time when he walked free: of hotel rooms heady with disinfectant, the clean but not-quite-bleached sheets in the two-bit hotels, La Chata and he traveling from one side of the country to the other, or across the border, to San Antonio, Texas, Guatemala, and that time in Tampico, as the sun went down over the Pánuco River, La Chata leaning against the balcony, facing the room, her body naked beneath a flimsy dressing gown and her legs slightly apart, her mound of Venus like a capital of hair atop the two columns of her thighs—it was impossible to resist, and Polonio, overcome by the same sensations as someone possessed by a religious trance, dropped to his knees to kiss it and sink his lips between hers. "They slip their finger in." Those mother-fuck-ing les-bian bit-ches. The Prick*'s* mother would carry the little packet of drugs *inside* her—despite the unforeseen changes to the original plan, what with them now being in the *hole*, the mother's task, as it were, remained the same—the little packet to feed her son's vice, just like before, in her belly, also inside her, she had fed him with life, with the horrible vice of living, of hauling oneself along, of crumbling like the Prick was crumbling, yet still relishing, to an indescribable degree, each and every morsel of life granted to him. Right now the Prick was draped around Polonio's neck begging to be allowed to look through the hatch; on his nape, below and behind his ear, Polonio felt the moist kiss of a purulent ulcer upon his skin, one of the Prick's unhealed wounds, the lips of an oyster kiss wetting him with a thin thread of saliva that ran down to his back, all because he didn't look after himself, all because of negligence, the hopeless miserable neglect to which he submitted himself. With his left hand, Polonio punched him in the stomach—a clumsy blow on account of his awkward position, his head poking through the hatch—and then kicked him lower down, far more effectively, sending him flying across the cell where he landed against the iron wall with a stunned and muffled cry. "Dickhead," the Prick grumbled, unperturbed and showing no hostility. "All I wanted was to see when my mami gets here." He spoke like a child, my *mami*, when he should have said my mother—my whore of a mother. For that's what she was. They'd had to come up with a new set of plans and the one in charge of executing them was Meche, Albino's girl. The women wouldn't come to visit *them*, but would instead use the names of other inmates, since their own men no longer had the right to visitors, not now they were *in the hole*. Albino was the most desperate of them all, maybe because he was the biggest, going so far as to weep from the lack of drugs, but stopping short of slitting his wrists, something all the addicts did when the anguish became too much. He had been a soldier, a sailor, and even a pimp—but not to Meche, she was no one's whore, she was an honorable woman, a slut for sure, but when she slept with other men it wasn't for money, no, it was purely for pleasure, behind Albino's back, of course. That's why she'd slept with Polonio so often. She was hot, absolutely smoking hot, but she was honorable, and to each her own. During their first days *in the hole* Albino distracted and entertained them—or rather he entertained Polonio, since the Prick remained hostile, listless, and incapable of understanding a fucking thing going on around him— with Albino's tremendous, rousing belly dance, renowned throughout the penitentiary, which caused such intense excitement that some, pointlessly trying to conceal their intentions, instead revealed their arousal and the coarse and harried sense of shame that threatened to engulf them, masturbating with furious and flagrant zeal, their hand under their clothes. It was a real privilege for Polonio to have watched him perform here, at his own leisure, in the cell, because elsewhere Albino provoked untold resentment as to who was allowed to join his audience; like any well-respected performer, he ejected all onlookers he considered inconvenient, frivolous, flippant, incapable of appreciating the hard-won attributes of a true virtuoso. Lower down his stomach was a tattoo of a Hindu figure—etched in the brothel of some Hindustani port, or so his story went, by the in-house eunuch, a member of an unpronounceable esoteric sect, while Albino dreamed a deep and almost lethal opium sleep beyond all possible recollection—the tattoo depicted an amusing couple, a young man and woman in the throes of passion, their bodies entwined, enlaced in an incredible foliage of thighs, legs, arms, breasts, and marvelous organs—the Brahmanic tree of Good and Evil—positioned in such a way and with such kinetic wisdom that Albino only had to set it in motion with the right contractions and muscle spasms, its rhythmic oscillations rising at intervals on the surface of his skin, and a subtle, inapprehensible rocking of the hips, for those flailing and capricious-looking body parts—torso and armpits, feet and pubis and hands and wings and stomachs and hair—to assume a mystical unity in which the miracle of the Creation was repeated and human copulation was portrayed in all its magnificent and marvelous splendor. In the cubicle where visitors were inspected before entering the prison, the hands of the female guard felt her through her dress—the finger would follow, the finger of God—but Meche's mind was elsewhere now: on Albino's dance to be exact, from the week before, in the visitors' lobby, just after they'd settled on the final details of the original plan, a plan they then abandoned on account of being sectioned in the *hole*, the Prick's mother also there, transfixed by the contortions of the tattoo, apparently confounded, but her lips drawn in a sly smile, and who, despite being well over sixty, was still well capable of making the beast with two backs, the old *mule*. In a corner of the room, hidden from prying eyes by a barrier of five people—the three women, the Prick, and Polonio—Albino had unfastened his trousers, his t-shirt now raised above his waist like a curtain to set the stage, using his mesmerizing stomach tremors to bring the coitus to life, emerging out of those inky blue lines with every step, with every rift and roll, every ripple and undulation, until all of them—except the Prick and his mother, who were doing their best to mask their reactions—felt a suffocating wave of desire course through their bodies, and, in Meche and La Chata's case, a brief and ambiguous giggle also danced on the roof of their mouths. Now naked from the waist down, Meche could anticipate the next moves of the guard's hand, something that had never happened to her before, disturbed by a strange and indecipherable willingness deep within her spirit and a half-hearted resistance, and in that moment Albino appeared in her imagination (in a previously forgotten memory, the first time they'd possessed each other, with intriguing new details now arising in her mind, absolutely fresh as if belonging to someone else), preventing her from assuming the proud indifference and fierce composure that she needed to withstand, patiently, angrily, coldly, the woman groping between her legs. For example, the heavy yet simultaneously repressed breathing, or rather irregular panting, neither steady nor erratic—only now did she realize it had all been air exhaled through his nose; Albino on top of her mound of Venus, for now the thumb and index finger of the female guard were already there, relentless, urgent, that female guard parting her lips, while suddenly, with the middle finger, she began a sweet, delicate, and highly suspicious internal exploration, a slow and deliberate in and out, the eyes utterly fixed as if unto death. The plan was for the women to enter the wing with the rest of the visitors, mingle with other prisoners' friends and families, and then appear unexpectedly at the door to the *hole*, willing to do anything to make the apes reconsider their men's punishment—refusing to move, standing firm for all time, like loyal, rabid she-dogs. The female guard, then, and her wandering hand, were the source of the double, triple, quadruple memories piling up and merging together, Meche at a loss to stop, remedy it, repress a dumb yet absolutely unavoidable attitude of acquiescence, which the bitch savored with a nervous quiver and fitful panting—almost ferocious, breathing only through her nose, actually just like Albino; at which Meche's own belly seemed to transform, indeed was transformed—by dint of a rebellious transposition—into *his* belly (Meche, good God, as if letting herself take the man's role in relation to the bitch) while the image of Albino seeped into her

latest sensations, scenes from their first performance, when he straddled her at eye-level, infus-
ing the figures from the Brahmanic tattoo with
spine-chilling and prodigious life, and now Meche
imagined that it was she who in that moment made
her belly dance—identical, albeit secret, invisible
undulations—like a seduction technique aimed at
the bitch, her eyes closing in, meaning that not
only did she not put up any resistance, but, without knowing why, impelled by the mysterious
force dictating these new internal relations between Albino, herself, and the guard—which
overtook those strangers by chance—she lay
down, barely metaphorically speaking (one word
would be enough to make her do it for real), in the
same position as that other Meche beneath Albino's body, completely and utterly intoxicated by
those Hindustani teenagers. Meche couldn't for-
mulate in any coherent or logical way, either in
words or in thoughts, what was happening to her:
what type of rarefied event and new language—secret, with exclusive and singular peculiarities—
was now being expressed, although it wasn't things
in general or taken all together, but rather each

thing separately, specifically, each thing apart, with their own words, emotions, and subterranean network of communications and significances, which connected them beyond time and space, regardless of the differences between them, so turning them into symbols and codes that were indecipherable to all those who fell outside of the biographical conspiracy by which things constituted themselves in their own particular hermetic disguise. Archaeology of passion, emotion, and sin, in which the weapons, tools, and abstract organs of desire and the tendency of every imperfect deed to seek out its consanguinity and completion in its own twin—however incestuous this may seem—get closer to their goal by means of a long, dogged, and tireless adventure of superimpositions, which slowly begin to assume the image of that whose form is but an unfulfilled yearning, condemned to be merely the nameless foundation of an eternally grasping proximity, restlessly clamoring signs that wait, febrile, for the moment when they finally unite with their twin meaning, and are decoded by their mere presence. So something—a face, a look, an expression, together constituting

the object's defining feature—is distilled and com-
plemented in another person, another love, and
even in other circumstances entirely, like archaeo-
logical horizons where details from each period—
a frieze, a gargoyle, an apse, a surround—are but
the moveable parts of a kind of despairing eternity
that time contracts, and where hands, feet, knees,
the way in which one looks at another, a kiss, a
stone, a landscape, through repetition are perceived by senses which no longer belong to that
then, even if the *past* refers to just a minute ago.
When Meche crossed the first barred door into the
yard leading onto numerous wings, radiating outward from a corridor, or rather a roundel, in the
center of which loomed the watchtower—a raised
iron polygon constructed to monitor every inch of
the prison from above—her mind was still imprinted with the image of the black and fatally elo-
quent eyes of the female guard, her motionless,
imperturbable, terrible eyes that might have been
staring at her forever. Polonio could no longer bear
to have his head lodged awkwardly against the
metal hatch, so he decided to cede his lookout post
to Albino, but, on shooting a sideways glance back

inside the cell, he thought he noticed a strange movement, and at just at the same instant he realized that the Prick had stopped moaning for the first time since being punched in the gut. Using great care and attention, slowly and cautiously, Polonio folded the ear poking through the hatch and drew back his head, worrying the whole time that Albino might have finally succeeded in choking the cripple. Truth to tell—he thought—there were more than enough reasons to do so, but Albino must keep his cool, at least for now, they would kill him under more favorable circumstances, as soon as the drugs were safely in their hands, not a moment earlier and not in that cell, since the plan might come crashing to the ground, and, whether they liked it or not, the Prick's mother was a vital part of the equation. It was a question of carefully planning where and how to kill him in the future (or the *not too distant* future, if that's what Albino wanted)—but all in good time. In reality, the Prick hadn't stopped moaning ever since Polonio had pummeled him in the stomach. His moans were irritating, repetitive, and ingeniously false, revealing quite openly and in perfect detail the mon-

strous state of his perverse, contemptible, despi-
cable, abject soul. The beating hadn't even been
that bad—his miserable body was used to even
more brutal and violent ones—so this phony anguish, affected purely to humiliate himself while
pleading for pity had the opposite effect, produc-
ing a mounting hatred and disgust, a blind rage
that unleashed the most lurid desires, from the
very depths of his heart, that he should suffer to
ridiculous extremes, that someone should inflict
more pain, real pain, capable of leaving him in
shreds (and here a childhood memory), just like a
malign tarantula, the same sensation that invades
the senses when the spider, under the effects of
boric acid, goes into a frenzy, shrivels into itself—
making a furious but impotent sound—curling up
inside its own legs, completely out of its mind, but
doesn't die, it doesn't die, and you'd like to squash
it but you don't have the energy for that, you don't
dare, and not being able to go through with it is
enough to drive you to tears. He whimpered in a
hoarse, weak, sticky voice, every now and then
feigning a woeful and shameless death rattle, while
with his tearful, dirty eye he managed to hold his

gaze still, a profoundly imploring gaze pierced with piety, full of self-pity, hypocrisy, falsehood, a distant malevolence. Polonio and Albino had only teamed up with the cripple because his mother was willing to help them, but once their business was done, he could go to hell, could go fuck himself, killing him was the only way out, the only way of recovering any peace or tranquility. "Leave him be!" Polonio barked at Albino, putting all his weight into giving him a hefty shove. Now released from Albino's clutches, the Prick was slumped like a lifeless sack in the corner. In fact, Albino had very nearly choked him to death, and now he didn't dare moan or kick up a fuss. Shaking and clumsily raising one hand to his chest, he rubbed his neck and massaged his Adam's apple between his fingers as if attempting to put it back in place. Now his one eye glinted in silent horror, so stupefied that suddenly he seemed unable to make sense of anything at all. The minute they pulled off the plan and the situation took a new turn, he planned to tell his mother—recounting all his terrible woes, and how nothing mattered to him, nothing *apart from* the small and fleeting pleasure, the sense of

calm the drug provided, and how, minute by minute and second by second, he was locked in battle
to find that peace, the only thing he loved in this
life, his only respite from the nameless torments he
endured and from the way he was forced, literally,
to trade his body's pain, piece by piece of his flesh,
in exchange for an indefinite and limitless interval
of freedom in which, with each fresh torture, he
floundered a little happier. Inserting—or extract-
ing—his head in and out of that iron rectangle,
back into the guillotine, moving his skull, with all
its parts—nape, forehead, nose, and ears—to the
world beyond the cell, placing it there just as you
would the head of a man sentenced to death, un-
real simply for still being alive, would require care-
ful, meticulous effort, the same way the fetus is
extracted from its maternal entrails, a tenacious
and deliberate self-birth with forceps that tear out
clumps of hair and scrape against skin. With Polonio's help, Albino was able to tilt his head at an
angle and position it on top of the metal sheet.
Down below were the *apes*, in the *box*, with all the
vacant and inexplicable primordial presence of
caged apes. Leaning his back against the door, next

to Albino's guillotined body, Polonio lit a cigarette and drew a long, deep drag into his lungs. The sun was falling across half the cell at an oblique, quadrangular angle, a solid, corporeal column inside whose glowing frame dust particles moved and collided with somnambular vagueness, erratic, distracted, confused, tracing the outline of a window of light with its vertical bars on the floor, not far from Polonio. Across from the solar buttress, the mute, resentful figure of the Prick blurred into the shadows. The billowing mountains of smoke exhaled by Polonio invaded the patch of light with an enveloping chaos of rumps, lips, legs, clouds, and the tumult of his personal cavalry, revolving and writhing in the hand-to-hand combat of shifting yet deliberate volumes of smoke, only then, slowly but surely, moving at the whim of the thick air, to settle with an easy and subtle rhythm on a horizontal plane, resembling a military victory parade. Then the movements shape-shifted to the rolling composition of other rhythms, and the slow, slow spirals paused briefly in their transitory state in poses of drunken idols and startled statues. Albino's voice reached him from beyond the iron

door—mild, confiding, tender. "Visiting time."
Visitors. Drugs. The bodies of smoke dissolved,
merged into one another, reconstructed reliefs
and structures and trails, subject to their own
laws—obedient to those of the solar system—now
wholly divine, free of all human traits, part of a
new and freshly invented natural world, whose
demigod was the sun, and where the nebulae, with
scarcely a whisper of geometry, before all Creation, occupied the freedom of a space that had
been formed in their own image and likeness, like
an immense, interminable desire that never per-
mits its own realization, nor does it describe its
own limits, refusing to be in any way contained,
just like God. But the Prick was still there, a bat-
tered, rotten anti-God, who began shaking with
the violent convulsions of a hacking, uncontrolla-
ble cough, which made him pound his body against
the wall—in a strange, spasmodic, and idiosyn-
cratic manner, beating out the dull, fleeting beat of
a bongo with a flabby drumskin. In the corner
where he sat huddled, he looked like a possessed
man, with his inflamed vulture's eye, verging on
asphyxiation. The lines, spirals, whorled snails,

statues, and gods gone mad were scattered, cracked, and banished by the spasms of that cough. He was missing one lung. Albino might have pressed his knee a little too hard against his chest when, moments earlier, he'd tried to throttle him. He really was a pain in the ass, this cripple. With considerable effort, Albino managed to squeeze his hand through the hatch, right up against his face, over the bridge of his nose, ready to grab the drugs at the moment that the women got up close to the cell. All of a sudden, he was blinded by a terrible rage: at the small moist scab, still not hardened, the pus from the Prick's open wound that the cripple must have left on Albino's hand during their scuffle, which Albino had been about to wipe on his lips. He closed his eyes, his head rattling the iron grid with the brute force of clenching his teeth. He was hell-bent on killing him, hell-bent with every atom of his soul. He opened his eyes to take another look. It wouldn't be long before the relatives started filing in. The padlocks had already been removed from both doors to the box in order to admit them, so the two groups were facing one another, on either side of the iron bars. *Their* women wouldn't file in as a group, but one at a time, mingling with the other visitors. Albino speculated as to who would appear first, La Chata, the mother, or Mercedes—Meche—with her beautiful body, shoulders, legs, angelic wings, all so enticing. (It was as if, under present circum-stances, the evocation of Meche was distorted by unforeseeable new factors full of contradictions, which lent the memory a different, original, strange quality: Meche had just been through an ordeal, the details of which Albino was none the wiser at that point, yet which, ever since he'd found out, a week before—when they plotted how to get the drugs into the penitentiary and Polonio had thought of using the Prick's mother—had re-mained imprinted on his mind, in various forms but always alluding to specific physical images. First of all, the clearly defined female guard, and then the diverse and unnerving meaning assumed by two words, who knows when or where Albino had heard them—exchanged between nurses or doctors as he'd waited someplace to be seen for whatever reason, this was all quite dreamlike, or perhaps it really was a dream—words which, given their convoluted technical character, encompassed a series of extensive and suggestive movements and situations: *gynecological position*. The female guard, and her method of searching one particular sector of the female visitors, not all of them, but a specific number who came to visit the drug addicts, and among them only the more active pushers inside the penitentiary: Albino and Polonio. Would they inspect the women in that *gynecological position*? The present situation—and those two absurd words—made this Meche slightly different from the usual Meche: violated and prostituted, not that this was a cause for repulsion, no, quite the opposite, a cause to feel closer to her, as if it lent her a natural, undefined loveliness, or at least one that Albino wasn't capable of defining; it didn't matter to him that Meche might have slipped into an unfortunate trance—and he would ask her himself, telling her to spare no details—in the event of a somewhat excessive exploration by the female guard during the inspection: it excited a renewed, previously unfamiliar desire in him, and a meticulous and honest retelling by Meche would give him hope, as they went on, for a new kind of bond to develop between them, more intense and complete, no doubt enjoying a healthy dose of lighthearted, happy depravity in which those two medical words would somehow play a role.) Although the "box" formed part of the wing, separated only by the same bars that acted as a barrier between the two of them, the presence of guards, shut up there inside, made it look like a separate prison, a prison for guards, a prison inside the prison, which visitors were obliged to pass through before entering the yard of the wing itself. This was Albino's entire field of vision from the hatch—a real torture. Being, as he was, taller than the peephole—chest-high to a man of normal height—Albino was forced to remain bent in a horribly awkward position to keep his head aligned at this angle, and after a couple of minutes he started to feel shooting pains down his neck and back, and his leg began to tremble, giving the ludicrous and mortifying impression that he was scared. As soon as one of the three women were through the first and second barred walls of the box—be it Meche, La Chata, or the mother—it was just a matter of doing something, anything—making a sound, kicking the door—to let them know exactly where the *hole* was. Naturally, the proper thing to do, he thought, would be to yell insults, hurl abuse at the *apes*. After all, that's what they were there for. The important thing was to see them enter, first the box and then the yard, to be sure that everything had gone smoothly during the inspection, with the *bitches*. Meche and La Chata wouldn't have had any trouble: the *apes* would have felt them up and that would've been that, nothing to find inside them. The mother was the important one. Please, please let the old hag through with those thirty grams tucked up her crack. For lack of a better word, they called what was about to happen a *strike*: a women's strike. But before Meche, La Chata and the mother went up there, to the cell door, so they could shout, scream, and stomp their feet, before the ruckus really kicked off, the mother was meant to hand over the little wrap of drugs to whoever had his head poking through the hatch. In this case Albino, the Baptist, was on duty, leaning his head against the metal plate. Later, *loaded up* on the drugs, he'd take care of the Prick. It was easy enough to pull off on movie night: deep in the shadows, drive the sharp end of an iron bar through his ribcage, while Polonio covered his mouth to stop him from squealing like a pig. They hadn't associated the Prick with him — or Polonio, precisely because of his baby face. Albino laughed: all because he had a mother. Having a mother was a big deal for that fucker, the real deal. The visitors formed a line in the central yard, not far away — all the same, beyond Albino's line of vision — before filing, one by one, onto the respective wings. Mothers, wives, daughters, young men, very few older men, two or three in each group, the air thick with suspicion, eyes down. Curiously enough, their conversations were never about why their relatives had been locked up. Nobody questioned the guilt or innocence of a child, husband, brother: they were there and that was that. The same couldn't be said for every visitor. Whenever some high-class lady set foot in the place, for the first few times at least, her sole, obsessive, and blatant concern — ultimately lacking all logic or even plain coherence — was to establish a clear social distinction between *her* inmate — why he was arrested, the temporary and purely incidental nature of his stay there in prison—and the rest of the visitors' inmates. Hers was merely "accused of," since no actual crime had been committed—no matter how shady things appeared—some friends in high places had been rallied in his favor, and two or three high-court judges were on the case. Those listening to her invariably nodded, incredulous but indulgent, going along with the *gran señora* who didn't pause for breath in her display of piously refined manners, who took their silence as wonder engendered by her ostentatiously luxurious attire. But as her presence in the line of visitors became more frequent, the lady of fine lineage gradually began to change her attitude, she began see things as they really were. Each time she would speak a little less of influential personages, and the innocence or guilt of "her" inmate noticeably dropped out of the conversation, as her outfits became plainer, until in the end she was just another visitor, eventually passing unnoticed, indistinguishable from the rest. La Chata spotted Meche behind her, among the other women in the line. She sighed. Oh, how she envied her. She really had it bad for Meche's man, Albino, and ever since he'd shown them his belly dance in the visitors' room, she went weak at the knees at the very thought of him. She would ask Meche if, without jeopardizing their friendship, she could sleep with Albino. Once or twice, that's all, no strings, or rather, without Meche getting all strung up about it. Further behind Meche, the Prick's mother hobbled in, looking suspicious. She'd let Meche and La Chata insert that contraceptive tampon as if it were nothing, with the indifference of a cow letting herself be milked. There were the udders; here was a vagina. Just as they'd predicted, she hadn't been searched. They'd shown some respect for her age, and the dairy cow passed through, as inoffensive as a virgin. But now they'd reached the *apes'* cage, the box. The Prick was pleading with them to let him poke his head through the hatch, because, he said, his mother wasn't going to hand over the drugs to anyone but him. But his pleas were feeble, despondent. Albino, with his head poking out of the cell, barked back at him. At last, Meche and La Chata appeared down below. "Those fucking *bitches*, stupid cunts!" The two women's eyes spun towards the voice: it was their man. But the old mule of a mother wasn't there—she was late, the wretch. The head in the guillotine flatly refused to give up the lookout post. His mother wasn't going to be so stupid as to give them the drugs, the Prick whined. Utter bullshit. Just like him to be pining to see his mother right here and now, needing her so desperately. He would tell her everything, not holding back like before. Everything. The interminable nights in the infirmary, strapped into a straightjacket, the ice-cold baths, the vein-cutting: of course he didn't want to die, but all the same he wanted to die—and the way he let himself go, let his body go like a loose thread, drifting, the boundless impiousness of human beings, his own infinite impiety, the evils of his cursed soul. Everything. He went on whining. "I told you to give it a fucking rest!" Just then the Prick's mother came through the two barred walls of the box and stepped into the yard in front of the wing. They were saved. Thanks to Albino's outburst, the women were able to make their way to the *holed* men's cell, transported as if by magic, invisible and swift, in a single movement, through the ebb and flow, the searching for one another in the crowd, in such a natural, confident, and self-possessed way that they didn't stand out or seem to have their own private agenda, so here they were already, just like that, and Meche had thrown herself at Holofernes's head and was showering it with kisses, on the ears, eyes, nose, smack on the lips. Helpless to escape, Albino merely flapped like the body of a monstrous fish, a fish with a human head, beached by a crashing ocean wave. "M'boy! W'is he?" cried the Prick's mother in a cavernous and somehow stupid voice; stupid because she seemed to be convinced that she would come face to face with her son right away, and when this didn't happen she became lost and confused, her expression full of fear and distrust toward the other two women. "W'is he? W'is he?" she repeated, lurching clumsily as if she were drunk, without taking her eyes off the head and hand protruding from the metal hatch. The head separated from the torso—guillotined and alive with its one visible eye rolling crazily, like what happens with cattle when they're thrown to the ground and know they're about to die—sent Meche and La Chata into a wild frenzy. Wild but also amused and merry, despite how deranged the whole situation was. They seemed younger than their years—they couldn't have been more than twenty-five—resembling a couple of teenage girls, sporty, bendy, agile, and as swaggering as they were vulgar. They'd climbed up onto the corridor handrail, and now sat with their legs crossed, feet clamped around the vertical bars, and from that position, skirts hitched high, exposing their thighs, they let out the most extraordinary howls and screeches, wildly flailing their clenched fists in the air, their toned arms like sturdy, steel roots, shaken by short, sharp electric shocks, while their eyes, open unnaturally wide, maddened and inflamed, glinted with unleashed rage. "Let them out, let them out," three words spliced into one furious emission: *leddemaat, leddemaat.* The mother didn't budge from between the two women. She clutched the handrail with both hands, as if on a ship's bridge, every now and then turning toward the yard and looking out of the corner of her eye in the direction of the hatch, hoping to see her son's head and not the other guy's, a man for whom she felt not the least affection or warmth. The head, now directly behind her, was spitting out demands with growing urgency, nearing hysteria. "The drugs, come on, old woman," sweetly at first, but with a note of aggression rapidly permeating his muted, restrained intonation. "The gear, you old hag! Give us the gear, you cunt!" It was quite possible that the mother really couldn't hear him. She looked like a stone slab, barely touched by a Neolithic tool—vast, heavy, solemn, and hideous. Her silence had something zoological, even lapidary about it, as if she lacked the organ necessary to make a single sound, to talk or shout, a beast mute from birth. All she did was weep, and even her tears filled you with the same horror as a strange animal seen for the first time, and for whom it is impossible to feel either compassion or love, just as was true of her son. Rather than falling vertically, the thick, slow tears slipped down her cheek along the old knife slash running from her forehead to her jaw, tracing the line of the scar, and then dripping from the tip of her chin—the tears were alien to her eyes, alien to the tears of all humanity. In the yard adjoining the prisoners' wing, with a subdued air of distraction, in vague need of something beyond themselves, something they found irresistible, the inmates and their relatives slowly gathered beneath the women perched on the rails. Nobody dared to yell or call out, but from the crowd there came a muffled buzzing, a unanimous hum of solidarity and satisfaction, which the *apes* couldn't pin on any one person. During visiting hours, the yard was transformed into a bizarre sort of campsite, with blankets spread across the floor and hung wall to wall between the cell doors, making a sort of temporary roof, beneath which each clan gathered, shoulder to shoulder—women, children, and inmates—in a kind of helpless throng of brutish castaways, strangers among strangers, or perhaps people who'd never had a home and today were practicing, entirely by instinct, a kind of warped, primitive cohabitation. Below the three women, the tide rose in small, slow successive waves, people congregating as if out on a stroll, the men never once averting their wide, cynical gaze, simultaneously expectant, amused and unnerved by Meche and La Chata's black panties. "Go on out then, you stupid *Prick*!" He didn't get it. "You, *you, get out there!*" Albino's head retreated arduously back into the cell allowing the mother to watch, almost immediately, exactly as if she were looking at herself in the mirror, how she gave birth to her son again, first the tousled, damp hair and then, bone by bone, forehead, cheekbones, jawbone, the flesh of her flesh, blood of her blood—dried up, bitter, and spent. She placed her tough, trembling hand on her son's forehead as if wanting to protect the blind eye from the intensity of the sun's rays. "The packet, Mami dearest, the packet you were going to bring," the man pleaded in a whining, desolate voice. Scared, speechless, sleepwalking in suffering, that hand resting instinctively on her son's forehead, all of a sudden she took on the hallucinatory and shocking likeness of a crudely-fashioned Our Lady of Sorrows, made of mud and stones and clay, unplaned and unpolished, an ancient, broken idol. Amid the increasingly frequent banging of muffled drums down below, a distinct isolated voice was calling out in chorus with the women. *Leddemaat, Leddemaat.* On their way from the Governor's office, a posse of ten guards entered the box. Nobody was prepared to take a risk: a path gradually cleared for those irregular and terrifying strides, *apes* released from captivity and still not used to running, above all wary of becoming separated from the group, from the tribe, not to end up caught in the middle of the stormy, impersonal crowd, acting with impunity, pretending not to see the *apes* pass, looking through them as if their bodies were transparent. The struggle against Meche, La Chata, and the old woman seemed to go on forever, a bloodless, painless, and somehow distant affair. Half-naked now, their clothes in shreds, they always found something, anything—a ledge, a crossbar, a fissure—to cling to, while three or four *apes* per woman made grotesque efforts to drag them toward the stairs. From the crowd's hoarse voice below erupted all sorts of exclamations, shouts, insults, and guffaws, some in protest, some in sympathy, and some savagely gleeful, demanding even more indecency, vulgarity, and shamelessness from the fabulous and once-in-a-lifetime spectacle that was all those bared breasts, asses, and midriffs. The mother, her short arms raised above her head, stood between the women and the *apes,* without doing a thing, making lumbering and labored jumps, like a fat old fowl who'd forgotten how to fly, a prehistoric link, not quite reptile, not quite bird. In the course of one of these jumps she tripped and went sliding across the iron surface of the walkway, only coming to a halt when her wide-open legs straddled a vertical bar of the handrail, preventing her, for now, from falling off the edge, but which wouldn't stop the other half of her body, suspended in mid-air, from plummeting into to the yard at any moment. There followed a roar of collective terror from everyone watching, followed by a suffocating, weird silence, as if there were not a single soul left on the face of the earth. The *holed* men, struck dumb in their cell and without having seen a thing, sensed that something immense was about to occur. The woman was beating her arms frantically, irrationally, flapping hard. "Don't move, old lady!" cried one of the *apes*, breaking the silence and dragging the mother from danger by her armpits. Silence returned, but now it was not only due to the absence of noise and voices, no, it was a silence that reigned over movements too, movements now entirely devoid of sound, wholly inaudible, as if all was a slow and imaginary underwater act performed by hypnotized divers, where everybody, actors and spectators alike, both present and far away, inhabited the diving suits of their own bodies, immobile and displacing their movements little by little, in stages, in autonomous and independent fragments, synchronized in their visible outward unity not by a causal and logical coherence, but precisely, by the icily rigid thread of madness. Something was stirring in this silent movie. Who knows what the Governor said to the *apes* and the women: an unfamiliar and tense calm descended, two *apes* bent down over the lock to the cell door and *unholed* the three recluses, and then the whole group—the three women, their men, and the guards—quietly, despite the crazed faces of Polonio, Albino, and even the Prick, began to head down the stairs. At the door to the box, the Governor let the two guards pass and then turned toward the women. He was quite sure his plan would work. "You can talk to your inmates in here all you like, under a watchful eye," he said. "Ladies first." The women obeyed with an air of weary victory. But they'd hardly stepped across the threshold when the first two *apes*, with lightning speed, pushed them back out of the box, through the other door that led out into the yard, immediately locking the door behind them. Suddenly, without warning, barely realizing what was happening, they'd been left behind on the other side of the wing, the other side of the world. The Governor didn't have time to laugh at his own ploy. In an unhinged, blind rage, Albino and Polonio, with the Prick between them, sprang forth unleashed, barging blindly and aggressively into the box, unwittingly followed by the Governor and another guard. In one abrupt gesture, Albino locked the door leading onto the wing. Now they were alone with the Governor and the three guards, captive in the same zoo cage. Four against three; no, two against four, given that the Prick was an absolute waste of space. "Let's see how you level with us now, you fucking ape pieces of shit," Albino yelled, while removing his cowhide belt to wield in the fight. A blow to the face, across his cheekbone and nose, suddenly caused a blood-red flower to bloom there, as if out of nowhere. Polonio and Albino transformed into two ancient gladiators, homicidal to the roots of their hair. The fight was hushed and precise, and as they prowled around the box not a single voice was raised, not a single groan heard. They were going for it, out to kill or wound their enemies in the most excruciating way possible, using their feet, fists, teeth, and sticks to tear out eyes and break their balls. Every look, expression, and gasp, every movement of an arm or a leg was calibrated, wholly sacrificed to the taut will of one unambiguously implacable goal, all of them oozing death in its fullest, most incredible manifestation. The women, powerless on the other side of the bars, screamed like demons, kicked out at whichever guard happened to be closest, and yanked the hair of anyone who momentarily toppled in their direction, pulling it out in great clumps, bleeding at the roots, often with whitish bits of hairy scalp attached. The mother was on her knees banging her forehead repeatedly against the floor, as if enacting an excessively outlandish prayer, while the Prick curled against the metal bars in a fervent attempt to shrink the volume of his body to an absolute minimum, howling endlessly, doing nothing but howling. More *apes* showed up from the Governor's office, at least twenty of them armed with very long metal poles. It was a matter of slotting the poles between the bars, rod by rod, from the grids on one side of the cage through to the other, and with the help of the guards who'd remained on the other side of the wing to hold them there, with two or three men securing each end, raising a line of barricades all the way across and up the rectangle, creating the most random and unpredictable arrangement of elevations and angles, as many as necessary to do battle against the two beasts, and at the same time mindful not to impede or thwart the actions of the Governor and the three *apes*, all in all a diabolical mutilation of the space, triangles, trapezoids, parallels, oblique or perpendicular divisions, lines and more lines, bars and more bars, until every possible move those gladiators could make was blocked and they were left crucified on the monstrous blueprint of this gargantuan defeat of liberty, all the fault of geometry. The first three of five horizontal bars perpendicular to the vertical ones flanking the box—primarily acting as supports for the poles which would be slotted from one side to the other, but also to sustain the vertical bars and thereby to structure the space—worked in the operation's favor: the lower bar, at knee height, and the middle and upper bars, which came up to just below the stomach and up to the neck of a man of average height respectively (although Albino's head towered above the tallest bar) meant that the *apes* could position the poles in such a way as to restrain that pair of crazed rebels, rendering them absolutely immobile. They, the gladiators, were invincible, higher than God, but this was too much for them. They tried to drive the poles upward, they jumped about and struggled in a thousand ways, but in the end they could do no more. The guards entered the cage to retrieve the Governor and his three helpers, who'd also been reduced to pieces. The women were dragged away, so hoarse their shouts had become inaudible. While all this was going on, the Prick managed to slide himself toward the feet of the officer who'd arrived with the guards. "Her," he whispered, gesturing toward his mother, with a sideways glance from his misty, teary eye, "it's her, she's who's carrying the drugs inside, up her crack, in her bits. Have her searched,

see for yourself." Only the officer heard. He smiled,
a sorry grimace. Hanging from the metal poles,
more captive than any captive, Polonio and Albino
resembled bloody rags, dismembered apes left out
to dry in the sun. All they knew for sure was that
the mother hadn't managed to hand the drugs to
her son, not to him, not to *no-ones*, as she would
say. It occurred to them both, in the same moment,
that there was no point in killing the cripple now.
Why bother.

LECUMBERRI PENITENTIARY
MEXICO, FEBRUARY–MARCH (15), 1969